For Sean and Fiona
- D.C.

For Ann, Hugh, Muriel and Breidge
- B.O'D.

For Pádraig
- R.M.

First published in Ireland by Discovery Publications,
Brookfield Business Centre, 333 Crumlin Road, Belfast BT14 7EA
Telephone: 028 9049 2410
Email address: declan.carville@ntlworld.com

Text © 2002 Declan Carville

Book Design © 2002 Bernard O'Donnell

Illustrations © 2002 Roisin Mathews

Declan Carville, Bernard O'Donnell and Roisin Mathews have asserted their rights to be identified as the author,
book designer and illustrator of this work under the Copyright, Designs and Patents Act, 1988.
No part of this publication may be reproduced or transmitted by any means, electronic, mechanical,
photocopying or otherwise without the prior permission of the publisher.

This story is based on Joe Mahon and Orlagh Bann's original screenplay for the Channel 4 series Sarah and the Whammi,
produced by Westway Films and funded by the Northern Ireland Community Relations Council and Channel 4.

A CIP catalogue record of this book is available from the British Library.

Printed in Ireland by Graham & Heslip.

ISBN 0-9538222-6-5

1 2 3 4 5 6 7 8 9 10

Sarah's Story

Declan Carville

illustrated by Roisin Mathews

book design by Bernard O' Donnell

Hello!

My name is Sarah and I'm going to tell you my story about the little bear in the woods.

This little bear was called 'Whammi'.
It had just been born and that was the only thing
it could say. The little bear felt very lonely and
wanted to find a family.
"Whammi!" it said.

The wood was full of
magic with a magic
wizard called Pointer.
Pointer promised the
little bear he would help it
all he could.

"Look, here is Davis.
Take his hand and he will
lead you through the
forest and help you find
your family."
But the little bear just
looked the other way.
"Why not take his hand,
little bear?" asked Pointer.
"He is only trying to help."

And so the little bear and Davis became friends and set off through the trees.

There were trees everywhere.
And what was that noise?

"Boo!" cried a group of blue bears. And they were waving sticks!

"Run!" shouted Davis, "as fast as you can!"

Puff!

And there was Pointer waving
his magic wand.
"Those bullies must be stopped.
Aren't you going to help Davis?"
he asked the little bear.
The little bear didn't know
what to do. It was very
confused and very frightened,
so it just ran away...

The little bear ran through the woods until it
came across some yellow bears.

"Whooppee!

This is fun!" the little bear thought to itself.
But the little bear was worried about Davis, though
it couldn't find anyone who wanted to help
catch those bullies. No one except Loribest, a new friend.
Side by side the little bear and Loribest set
off through the woods.

"Look! There's Davis locked up in a cage!" exclaimed the little bear.
"We had to lock him up because he was causing trouble," said one of the guards.
"There's been a terrible mistake! It was the blue bears who bullied Davis!" said the little bear. When they told the guards what had really happened, they set Davis free.

Up and down. High and
low. They searched
everywhere for a family
for the little bear.
"I'm hungry," said Loribest.
"Let's find something nice
to eat!"
"We could go to the
Food Wood," said Davis.

Puff!

And there was Pointer.
"Not you, little bear" said
the wise old Wizard.
"There is something I'd like
you to do..."

The little bear was not very happy. It wanted to go with
the others. So it just sat down in the middle of the woods.
"*Ohhhhhhh!*" groaned the tree.
"What a sad face," thought the little bear. "I know what I'll do..."

The little bear started to clear away some of the weeds
from around the big old tree and then it sprinkled a little water
with the watering can.
Wow! What a difference!
Cakes and buns and so many good things to eat!
"Ahh!" said the little bear patting its tummy. "Delicious!"

On the way back to find Davis and Loribest, the little bear came across some purple bears swinging through the trees. "You can't join in!" shouted one of the purple bears. "You're not one of us."

Puff! And there was Pointer. "We may not look the same, but we must all learn to share," said Pointer. And so everybody joined in the fun.

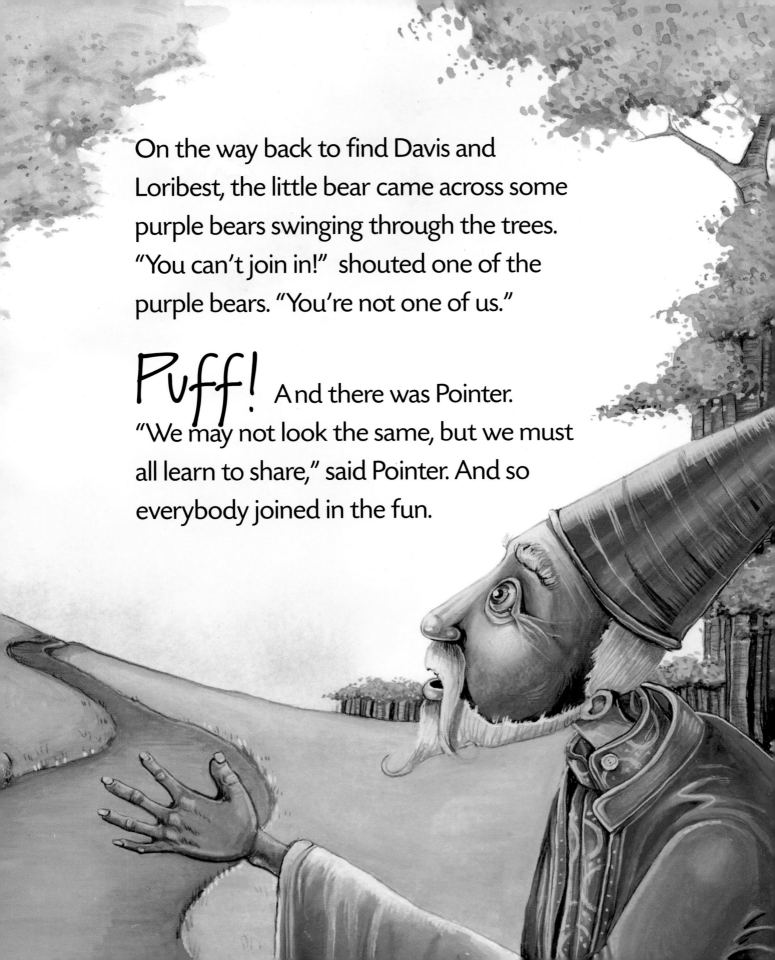

Now every magic wood has a Little Princess,
and this one had a magic wand as well.
"I don't want you around here anymore!"
she said.
Whooshh! And they were gone!

The Little Princess was doing just
as she wanted. She didn't care
about anybody else except herself.

Oh dear! Pointer wasn't very pleased!

Puff! And the wise old Wizard was back.

"Naughty, naughty!" he scolded.

And in a puff of smoke she disappeared!

"We mustn't delay" said Loribest, "we still need to find you a family."

"No need," said Pointer, "they are here already."

Everybody was invited. At last the little bear had found what it had been looking for.

Everyone must learn to treat others the right way too!

Enjoy more great picture books from Discovery Publications

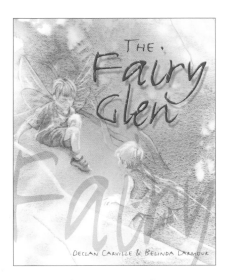

The Fairy Glen

Declan Carville &
Belinda Larmour
ISBN 09538222-3-0

Boo!!! said the Banshee

Declan Carville &
Kieron Black
ISBN 0-9538222-5-7

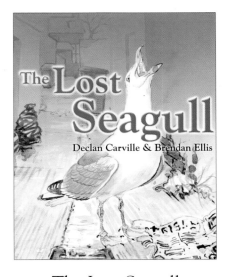

The Lost Seagull

Declan Carville &
Brendan Ellis
ISBN 0-9538222-4-9

A Day to Remember at the Giant's Causeway

Declan Carville &
Brendan Ellis
ISBN 09538222-0-6

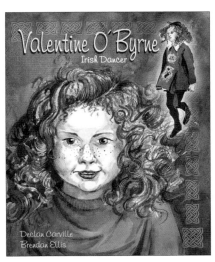

Valentine O'Byrne Irish Dancer

Declan Carville &
Brendan Ellis
ISBN 09538222-1-4

The Incredible Sister Bridget

Declan Carville &
Kieron Black
ISBN 09538222-2-2